GULLIVER'S TRAVELS

" My arms and legs were fastened to the ground."

(SEE PAGE 15)

GULLIVER'S TRAVELS
IN LILLIPUT AND BROBDINGNAG

———

FROM THE STORY BY
DEAN SWIFT

Illustrated by Will Nickless

BLACKIE
LONDON AND GLASGOW

BLACKIE & SON LIMITED
5 FITZHARDINGE STREET
PORTMAN SQUARE
LONDON · W.I
BISHOPBRIGGS, GLASGOW

BLACKIE & SON
(INDIA) LIMITED
103-5 FORT STREET
BOMBAY

PRINTED IN GREAT BRITAIN BY BLACKIE & SON LIMITED · GLASGOW

CONTENTS

A VOYAGE TO LILLIPUT

✑ A Voyage to Lilliput ✍

I HOW GULLIVER WAS MADE PRISONER

My father had a small estate in Nottingham-shire. I was the third of five sons. At the age of fourteen I went to Cambridge University, where I remained for three years, and applied myself closely to my studies. As my father could not keep me longer there, I went to London and became a surgeon.

As success did not attend me, I engaged myself as a surgeon on a ship, and after making a voyage or two I returned to London and settled there for some time. I had a good practice at first, but this dwindled till I was forced to give it up. I again made up my mind to go to sea. I was surgeon in two ships, and made several voyages, for six years, to the East and West Indies, by which I got some addition to my fortune.

The last of these voyages not proving very fortunate, I grew weary of the sea, and intended to stay at home with my wife and family. But after three years I engaged myself as surgeon on the good ship *Antelope*, which was making a voyage to the South Sea. We set sail from Bristol, May 4, 1699, and our voyage at first was very prosperous.

It would not be proper, for some reasons, to trouble the reader with the whole story of our adventures in these seas. Let it be enough to inform him that in our passage from the South Sea to the East Indies we were driven by a violent storm to the north-west of Van Diemen's Land. Twelve of our crew died through hard work and the want of food. The rest were in a very weak condition.

On the 5th of November, which was the beginning of summer in those parts, the weather being very hazy, the seamen spied a rock within half a cable's length of the ship. But the wind was so strong that we were driven upon the rock, and the vessel split in two.

Six of the crew, of whom I was one, having let down a boat into the sea, tried hard to get clear of the ship and the rock. We rowed about three leagues, till we were able to work no longer, for we were already much spent with the hard work we had had on board the ship.

We therefore trusted ourselves to the mercy of the waves, but in about half an hour the boat was overturned by a sudden squall of wind. I cannot tell what became of my companions in the boat, or of those who escaped on to the rock or were left in the vessel. But I think they were all lost.

For my own part, I swam as fortune directed me, and was driven along by the wind and the tide. I often let my legs drop, but could not feel the bottom. When I was almost gone, and not able to struggle any longer, I found myself within my depth. By this time the storm had nearly passed.

The slope was so gradual that I walked nearly a mile before I got to the shore. It was about eight o'clock in the evening when I reached dry land. I was very tired, and, the weather being very warm, I felt myself much inclined to sleep. I lay down on the grass, which was very short and soft. There I slept sounder than I ever remember to have done in my life. I must have slept nine hours, for, when I awoke, it was just daylight.

I attempted to rise, but was not able to stir. For, as I happened to lie on my back, I found my arms and legs were strongly fastened on each side to the ground. My hair, which was long and thick, was tied down in the same way. I likewise felt several slender threads across my body. As I could only look upwards, and the sun began to grow hot, the light hurt my eyes. I heard a confused noise about me, but, in the position in which I lay, I could see nothing except the sky.

In a little while I felt something alive moving on my left leg. It advanced gently forward over my breast, and came almost up to my chin. When I cast my eyes downward as far as I could, I saw it to be a human creature scarcely six inches high, with a bow and arrow in his hands, and a quiver on his back.

In the meantime I felt at least forty more of the same kind following the first. I was greatly astonished, and roared so loud that they all ran back in a fright. Some of them, as I was afterwards told, were hurt by the falls they got in leaping from my sides to the ground. However, they soon returned, and one of them ventured so far as to get a full view of my face. When he saw it, he lifted up his hand and eyes, and cried out in a strange language, of which I knew not a word.

I lay all this time in great distress. At length, struggling to get free, I had the good fortune to break the strings, and pull out the pegs, which fastened my left arm to the ground. By lifting my arm to my face I found out the methods they had taken to bind me. With a violent pull which gave me great pain, I loosened a little the strings that tied down my hair on the left side, so that I was just able to turn my head about two inches.

Before I could seize the creatures, they ran off a second time. Then there was a great shout, and after it ceased I heard one of them cry out aloud in the same language as before. In an instant I felt above a hundred arrows discharged on my left hand. They pricked me like so many needles. Besides, the creatures shot a number into the air, many of which fell on my body, and some on my face.

When this shower of arrows was over, I groaned with pain and grief. On my again striving to get free, they discharged another volley more numerous than the first, and some of them tried to stick me with spears in the side. By good luck I had on a buff jerkin, which they could not pierce.

I thought it best to lie still. My plan was to continue so till night, when, my left hand being already loose, I could easily free myself. I had reason to believe that I might be a match for the greatest army they could bring against me, if they were all of the same size as the one I saw.

But fortune disposed of me otherwise. When the people observed I was quiet, they discharged no more arrows. By the noise I heard, I knew that their numbers had increased. About four yards

from me I heard a knocking for more than an hour, as if some people were at work. When I turned my head in the direction of the noise, as well as the strings and pegs would permit me, I saw a wooden stage erected about a foot and a half high, capable of holding four of the inhabitants. From this stage one of them made me a long speech, of which I knew not a word.

Before he began to speak, however, I should have said that he gave orders to cut the strings that fastened the left side of my head. This enabled me to turn it to the right and to see the person who was speaking. He appeared to be of middle age, and taller than any of the other three who attended him, one of whom was a page that held up his train, and seemed a little longer than my middle finger. The other two stood one on each side to support him.

With some difficulty I made him understand that I knew nothing of what he and the others said, but that I wished them no harm. Being almost starved with hunger, for I had not eaten a morsel for some hours before I left the ship, I showed them by putting a finger of my left hand often into my mouth that I wanted food. The great lord on the stage understood me very well.

He at once came down and commanded that several ladders should be set up against my sides. On these more than a hundred of the inhabitants mounted. They walked towards my mouth, laden with baskets full of meat, which had been provided and sent thither by the King's orders, upon the first news he received of me.

I observed there was the flesh of several animals but I could not make them out by the taste. There were shoulders, legs, and loins, shaped like those of mutton, and very well dressed, but smaller than the wings of a lark. I ate them by two or three at a mouthful, and took three loaves at a time, about the size of musket bullets. They supplied me as fast as they could, and showed a thousand marks of wonder and surprise at my bulk and at the amount I ate.

I then made another sign, that I wanted drink. They found by my eating that a small quantity would not satisfy me. So, being a very clever people, they slung up, with great skill, one of their largest hogsheads. They rolled it towards my hand, and beat out the top of it. I drank it off at a draught, which I might well do, for it did not hold half a pint, and tasted like wine, but was much more delicious.

They brought me a second hogshead, which I drank in the same way, and then made signs for more. But they had none to give me. When I had performed these wonders, they shouted for joy, and danced upon my breast. They made me a sign that I should throw down the two hogsheads, but they first warned the people below to stand out of the way. When they saw the vessels in the air, there was a great shout.

I confess I was often tempted, while they were passing backwards and forwards on my body, to seize forty or fifty of the first that came within

my reach, and dash them to the ground. But the
remembrance of what I had felt, which perhaps
might not be the worst they could do, and the
promise of honour I had made them, soon drove
out these thoughts. I could not but wonder at the
courage of these very little mortals, who dared
to mount and walk on my body, while one of my
hands was free, without trembling at the sight of
so large a creature as I must appear to them.

After some time, when they observed that I
made no more demands for food, there appeared
before me a person of high rank, from the
Emperor. Having mounted on the small of my
right leg, he advanced forwards up to my face,
with about a dozen of his followers. For about
ten minutes he spoke to me without any signs of
anger, but with a firm look on his face. He often
pointed forwards, which, as I afterwards found,
was towards the capital city, about half a mile
distant. It had been agreed by the Emperor that I
was to be taken there.

I answered in a few words, but to no purpose.
I made a sign with the hand that was loose,
putting it to the other, and then to my head and
body, to show that I wished to be freed from my
bonds. It appeared that he understood me well
enough, for he shook his head by way of refusal,
and held his hand in such a way as to show that I

must be carried as a prisoner. However, he made other signs to let me know that I should have meat and drink, and should be very well treated.

Upon this I once more thought of attempting to break my bonds. But when I felt the smart of their arrows upon my face and hands, which were all in blisters, and in which many of the darts were still sticking, I gave tokens to let them know that they might do with me what they pleased. Soon after I heard a general shout, and I felt great numbers of people on my left side freeing the cords to such a degree that I was able to turn upon my right side, and to ease myself.

But before this they had daubed my face and both my hands with a sort of ointment, which was very pleasant to the smell, and in a few minutes removed all the smarts of their arrows. This, added to the refreshment I had received by their food and drink, which were very, very nourishing, caused me to fall asleep. I slept about eight hours, as I was afterwards told. And it was no wonder, for in the wine that had been given me to drink there was mixed a draught of something which always caused deep sleep.

It seems that upon the first moment I was discovered sleeping on the ground, after my landing, the Emperor had received early notice of it. He determined, in council, that I should be tied in the manner in which I have related (which was done in the night while I slept). Plenty of food and drink was to be sent me and a machine prepared to carry me to the capital city.

This plan, perhaps, may appear very bold and dangerous, and I feel sure would not be imitated by any prince in Europe on a like occasion. However, in my opinion it was very prudent, as well as generous. If these people had tried to kill me with their spears and arrows while I was asleep, I should certainly have been awakened with the first feeling of smart. This might so far have roused my rage and strength as to have enabled me to break the strings with which I was tied. And as they would not have been able to resist me, so they could not have expected mercy.

These people are very clever, and are encouraged by the Emperor, who is a renowned patron of learning, and they have become very skilful in their work. This prince has several machines fixed on wheels, for the carrying of trees and other great weights. He often builds his largest men-of-war, of which some are nine feet in length, in the woods, where the timber grows, and has them carried on these engines three or four hundred yards to the sea.

But none of his carriages were large or strong enough to carry me; so five hundred carpenters

and engineers were set to work to prepare the
greatest engine they could. It was a frame of
wood, raised three inches from the ground, about
seven feet long, and four wide, moving on
twenty-two wheels. The shout I heard was upon
the arrival of this engine, which it seems set out
four hours after my landing.

This huge carriage was brought alongside of
me as I lay. But the great difficulty was to raise
and place me in the carriage. Eighty poles, each
of which was one foot high, were erected for this
purpose, and very strong cords, of the thickness
of pack-thread, were fastened by hooks to many
bandages, which the workmen had tied round my
neck, my hands, my body, and my legs. Nine
hundred of the strongest men then drew up these
cords by means of many pulleys fastened on the
poles. In this way, in less than three hours, I was
raised and placed in the engine, and there tied
fast.

All this I was told. For, while the work was
being done, I lay in a deep sleep, by the force of
that sleepy potion put into the wine I had drunk.
Fifteen hundred of the Emperor's largest horses,
each about four inches and a half high, were
employed to draw me to the city, which, as I said,
was half a mile distant.

About four hours after we began our journey,

I was awakened by a very strange accident. The carriage stopped for a few minutes to repair something that was out of order, and two or three of the young natives were very curious to see how I looked when I was asleep. They climbed up into the engine, and advanced very softly to my face. One of them, an officer of the guards, put the sharp end of his half-pike a good way up into my left nostril, and this tickled my nose like a straw, and made me sneeze violently. Upon this they stole off without being seen, and it was three weeks before I knew the cause of my waking so suddenly.

We made a long march the remaining part of the day, and rested at night with five hundred guards on each side of me, half of them with torches, and the other half with bows and arrows, ready to shoot me if I should offer to stir. The next morning, at sunrise, we continued our march, and arrived about noon within two hundred yards of the city gates. The Emperor and all his Court came out to meet us, but his great officers would not allow His Majesty to put his person in danger by mounting on my body. At the place where the carriage stopped there stood an ancient temple, esteemed to be the largest in the whole kingdom. This temple had not been used for some years, as a murder had taken place in it. In this building it was decided that I should lodge. The great gate fronting to the north was about four feet high, and almost two feet wide, and I could easily creep through it. On each side of the gate was a small window, not above six inches from the ground.

Into the window on the left side the Emperor's smiths carried fourscore and eleven chains, like those that hang to a lady's watch in Europe, and almost as large. They locked these to my left leg with six and thirty padlocks.

Over against this temple, on the other side of the great highway, at a distance of twenty feet, there was a turret at least five feet high. Here the Emperor ascended, with many of the chief lords of his Court, to have a view of me, as I was told, for I could not see them. About a hundred thousand people came out of the town for the same purpose. In spite of my guards, I believe there could not be fewer than ten thousand who at several times mounted my body by the help of ladders. But after a while this was forbidden on pain of death.

When the workmen found it was impossible for me to break loose, they cut all the strings that bound me. Upon this I rose up as sad as ever I was in my life. But the noise and surprise of the people at seeing me rise and walk cannot be described. The chain, which was about two yards long and held my left leg, gave me the liberty of walking backwards and forwards in a half-circle. As it was fixed within four inches from the gate, it allowed me to creep in and lie at full length in the temple.

2   HOW GULLIVER MADE FRIENDS

When I found myself on my feet, I looked about me, and must confess I never beheld a more beautiful sight. The country round about appeared like one large garden, and the enclosed fields, which were generally forty feet square, seemed to be so many beds of flowers. In these fields were woods, the tallest trees of which, as far as I could judge, appeared to be seven feet high. I had a view of the town on my left hand, which looked like the painted scenes of a city in a theatre.

The Emperor then descended from the tower, and advanced on horseback towards me. This very nearly cost him dear. For his horse, though very well trained, was so unused to such a sight, which appeared as if a mountain moved before him, that he reared up on his hind feet. But the

Emperor, who is an excellent horseman, kept his seat till his servants ran in and held the bridle, while His Majesty had time to dismount.

When he got off his horse, he looked me all round with great admiration, but he kept beyond the length of my chain. He ordered his cooks to give me food and drink. They pushed these forward in a sort of machine upon wheels, till I could reach them. I took these machines and soon emptied them all. Twenty of them were filled with food and ten with drink. Each of the former gave me two or three good mouthfuls. I emptied the drink of ten earthen vessels into one large one and drank it off at a draught.

The Empress, and the young Princes and Princesses, attended by many ladies, sat in their chairs at some distance. But upon the accident to the Emperor's horse they got down, and came near the Emperor, whom I am now going to describe.

He was taller, by almost the breadth of my nail, than any of his Court. This alone was enough to strike an awe into the beholders. His features were strong and masculine, with an Austrian lip and arched nose, his body and limbs were well proportioned and all his movements graceful. He was then a little past his prime, being twenty-eight and three-quarter years old. He had reigned in great happiness for about seven years and had been generally victorious.

That I might the better see him, I lay on my side, so that my face was alongside of his. He stood only three yards off. However, I have had him many times in my hand since, and therefore my description of him is correct.

His dress was very plain and simple. He had on his head a light helmet of gold, adorned with jewels, and a plume on the crest. He held his sword drawn in his hand to defend himself, if I should happen to break loose. This sword was about three inches long. The hilt and the sheath were of gold enriched with diamonds. His voice was shrill, but very clear, and I could distinctly hear it when I stood up.

The ladies and courtiers were all most beautifully dressed, so that the spot upon which they stood looked as if it were a cloth spread on the ground and embroidered with figures of gold and silver.

The Emperor spoke often to me and I returned answers, but neither of us could understand a single word. In attendance upon the Emperor were several priests and lawyers, at least they appeared to be so by their dress. The Emperor commanded them to address themselves to me. I spoke to them in all the languages of which I had the least smattering, some of which were English, Dutch, Latin, French, Spanish, and Italian, but it was all to no purpose.

After about two hours the Court retired, and I was left with a strong guard to prevent the rabble coming too close to me. Some of the crowd, however, shot their arrows at me, as I sat on the ground by the door of my house. One of the arrows very narrowly missed my left eye. The colonel ordered six of the ringleaders to be seized; and thinking they would be properly punished if they were handed over to me, he commanded the soldiers to push them forward with the butt-ends of their pikes, until they were within reach of me. I then took them all up in my right hand.

Five of them I put into my coat pocket, and the sixth I raised up to my mouth, as if I would eat him alive. The poor man screamed out loudly. The colonel and his officers became much alarmed especially when they saw me take out my pen-knife. But I at once put them out of fear by looking mildly at them, and, cutting the strings with which the prisoner was bound, I set him gently on the ground, and away he ran.

I treated the rest of them in the same way, taking them one by one out of my pocket. I observed that both the soldiers and the people

were highly delighted at this mark of my mercy, and I found that my conduct in this matter was highly spoken of at the Court.

Towards night I got with some difficulty into my house, where I lay on the ground, and continued to do so for about a fortnight. During this time the Emperor gave orders to have a bed prepared for me. Six hundred beds of the ordinary size were brought in carriages, and worked up in my house. The workmen laid them upon the floor in four layers, a hundred and fifty of their beds being sewn together to make the breadth and the length. Even then they were hardly thick enough to keep me from the hardness of the floor, which was of smooth stone. In the same way they provided me with sheets, blankets, and coverlets, which were good enough for one who had been so long used to hardships.

As the news of my arrival spread through the kingdom, it brought great numbers of rich, idle, and curious people to see me. If the Emperor had not issued orders against it, the tilling of the land and all household work would have been everywhere neglected, and the villages would almost have been emptied. Therefore he directed that those who had already seen me should go home, and not presume to come within fifty yards of my house, without leave from the Court.

In the meantime the Emperor held frequent meetings to discuss what should be done with me. I was afterwards assured by a particular friend, a person of great quality, who was as much in the secret as any, that the Court had great difficulties in the matter. They were afraid that I would break loose, or that the amount of food I required would cause a famine. Sometimes they determined to starve me, or at least to shoot me in the face with poisonous arrows and thus kill me.

In the midst of these discussions, several officers of the army went to the door of the great meeting-place, and, two of them being admitted, gave an account of how I had behaved to the six prisoners mentioned above. This made so favourable an impression on the Emperor that orders were given to all the inhabitants of the villages, nine hundred yards round the city, to deliver every morning six oxen, forty sheep, and other food for my support, together with a large quantity of bread and wine.

The Emperor paid for all this out of his own purse, for he lives chiefly upon his own income. Seldom, except upon great occasions, does he raise any money from his own subjects, who are bound to attend him in his wars at their own expense. Six hundred servants were also given me,

3   (H 757)

who had board wages allowed them, and tents
built for them on each side of my door.

It was likewise ordered that three hundred
tailors should make me a suit of clothes, after the
fashion of the country. The Emperor also commanded that six of his greatest scholars should be
engaged to teach me the language of the country.
He ordered that the royal horses should be
frequently exercised in front of me, so that they
might become accustomed to me.

All these orders were duly carried out. In three
weeks I had made great progress in learning their
language. During that time the Emperor frequently honoured me with his visits, and was
pleased to assist my masters in teaching me. We
began to converse together in some sort of way.
The first words I learnt were used to express my
desire that he would be pleased to give me my
liberty. This I repeated every day on my knees.
His answer, as far as I could make it out, was, that
this must be a work of time, and not to be
thought of without the advice of his council, and
that first I must enter into a treaty of peace with
him and his kingdom. However, he promised that
I should be used with all kindness.

He advised me, too, to gain by my patience
and discreet conduct the good opinion of himself
and his subjects. He desired that I would not take

it ill if he gave orders to certain officers to search
me. For perhaps I carried about on me weapons,
which might be dangerous things if they corres-
ponded to the size of so large a person.

I answered that His Majesty should be satisfied,
as I was ready to strip myself and turn out my
pockets before him. This answer I gave partly in
words and partly by signs. He replied that by the
laws of the kingdom I must be searched by two of
his officers. He knew, he said, that this could not
be done without my consent and help. He had so
good an opinion of my kindness and justice that
he would trust their persons in my hands. Whatever they took, he said, should be returned when
I left the country, or paid for at the rate at which
I valued it.

I took up the two officers in my hands, and put
them first into my coat pockets and then into
every other pocket I had, except my two fobs.
Another secret pocket I had I did not let them
search, since it had needful things that were of no
consequence to anyone but myself. In one of my
fobs there was a silver watch, and in the other a
small quantity of gold in a purse.

These gentlemen, having pens, ink, and paper
about them, made an exact list for the Emperor
of everything they saw. When they had done this,
they desired that I would set them down that

they might deliver the list to the Emperor. This list I afterwards translated into English, and it is as follows:

'In the right coat pocket of the great Man-Mountain, after the strictest search, we found only one great piece of coarse cloth, large enough to cover the floor of Your Majesty's chief Room of State. In the left pocket we saw a huge silver chest, with a cover of the same metal, which we, the searchers, were not able to lift. We desired that it should be opened, and one of us, stepping into it, found himself in a sort of dust. Some of this dust flew up into our faces and set us both a-sneezing for several times together.

'In his right waistcoat pocket we found a very large bundle of a thin, white substance, folded one over another, about the size of three men. These are tied with a strong cable, and marked with black figures, which we humbly conceive to be writings, every letter almost half as large as the palm of our hands.

'In the left pocket there was a sort of engine, from the back of which were extended twenty long poles, like the palings before Your Majesty's Court. With this we think the Man-Mountain combs his hair, for we did not always trouble him with questions, because we found it very difficult to make him understand us.

'In the large pocket on the right side of his breeches we saw a hollow pillar of iron, about the length of a man, fastened to a strong piece of timber larger than the pillar. Upon one side of the pillar were huge pieces of iron sticking out, cut into strange figures, which we know not what to make of.

'In the left pocket was another engine of the same kind. In the smaller pocket on the right side were several round flat pieces of white and red metal, of different sizes. Some of the white pieces, which seemed to be of silver, were so large that my comrade and I could hardly lift them.

'In the left pocket were two black pillars irregularly shaped. We could not without great difficulty reach the top of these, as we stood at the bottom of his pocket. One of them was covered, and seemed as if it were one piece, but at the upper end of the other there appeared a white round substance about twice the size of our heads. Within each of these was a huge plate of steel. We ordered him to show us them, for we feared that they were dangerous weapons. He took them out of their cases, and told us that, in his own country, his practice was to shave his beard with one of these, and cut his food with the other.

'There were two pockets which we could not enter. These he called his fobs. They were two large slits cut into the top of his breeches and pressed close together. Out of the right fob hung a great silver chain, with a wonderful kind of engine at the bottom.

'We directed him to draw out whatever was at the end of that chain. It appeared to be a globe, half of silver and half of some metal through which you can see. On the transparent side we saw strange figures drawn in a circle. We thought we could touch them, till we found our fingers stopped by this strange metal.

'He put this engine to our ears, and we found that it makes a terrible noise, like that of a water mill, and this is unceasing. We think it is either some unknown animal, or the god that he worships. We are more inclined to believe it is his god, for he assured us (if we understand him right, for he expressed himself imperfectly) that he seldom did anything without consulting it. He called it his oracle, and said it pointed out the time of every action of his life.

'From the left fob he took out a net, almost large enough for a fisherman, which opened and shut like a purse, and served him for the same use. In it we found several large pieces of yellow metal, which, if they be real gold, must be of immense value.

'Having thus, in obedience to Your Majesty's

commands, diligently searched all his pockets, we observed a girdle about his waist made of the hide of some huge animal. From it, on the left side, hung a sword of the length of five men. On the right of it hung a bag or pouch divided into two cells, each cell capable of holding three of Your Majesty's subjects.

'In one of these cells were several globes or balls of a very heavy metal, about the size of our heads, and which required a strong hand to lift them. The other cell contained a heap of certain black grains, but of no great size or weight, for we could hold above fifty of them in the palms of our hands.

'This is an exact list of what we found about the body of the Man-Mountain, who used us very kindly and paid great respect to the orders of Your Majesty. Signed and sealed on the fourth day of the eighty-ninth month of Your Majesty's happy reign:

CLEFRIN FRELOCK
MARSI FRELOCK.'

When this list was read over to the Emperor, he directed me, although in very gentle terms, to deliver up all the articles named in it. He first called for my sword, which I took out, sheath and all. In the meantime, he ordered three thousand of the choicest troops (who then attended him) to surround me at a distance with their bows and arrows just ready to shoot. But I did not observe them, for my eyes were fixed upon His Majesty.

He then desired me to draw my sword, which, although it had got some rust by the sea water, was in most parts very bright. I did so, and immediately all the troops gave a shout between terror and surprise. For the sun shone clear, and the reflection dazzled their eyes, as I waved the sword to and fro in my hand. His Majesty, who is a most generous prince, was far braver than I could expect. He ordered me to put the sword back into the scabbard, and to throw it on the ground, as gently as I could, about six feet from the end of my chain.

The next thing he demanded was one of the hollow iron pillars, by which he meant my pocket pistols. I drew it out, and at his desire, as well as I could, told him the use of it. I filled it only with powder, which, by the closeness of my pouch, happened to escape being wet in the sea, and first telling the prince not to be afraid, I let it off in the air. The surprise in this case was much greater than at the sight of the sword, for hundreds of people fell down as if they had been struck dead. Even the Emperor, although he stood his ground, could not recover himself for some time.

I delivered up both my pistols in the same way as I had done my sword, and then my pouch of powder and bullets. I begged him to keep the powder from the fire, for it would kindle with the smallest spark and would blow up the royal palace into the air. I also gave up my watch, which the Emperor was very curious to see. He commanded two of his tallest yeomen of the guard to bear it on a pole upon their shoulders. He was amazed at the constant noise it made and at the movement of the minute hand, which, since his sight is much keener than ours, he could easily see.

He then asked the opinions of his learned men about it. These opinions were very different and far from right, as the reader may well imagine without my telling them. I could not very well understand, however, all they said.

I then gave up my silver and copper money, and my purse with the nine large pieces of gold and some smaller ones. My knife and razor, my comb and silver snuff-box, my handkerchief and journal book were also all delivered up. My sword, pistols and pouch were conveyed in carriages to His Majesty's stores. But the rest of my goods were given back to me.

I had, as I before observed, one private pocket, which escaped their search. In it there was a pair of glasses (which I sometimes use because of the weakness of my eyes), a pocket glass, and some other little objects. As these were of no consequence to the Emperor, I did not think myself bound in honour to show them, and I feared lest they might be lost or spoiled, if I let them out of my hands.

3   THE COURT AT LILLIPUT

My gentleness and good conduct had gained so far on the Emperor and his Court, and indeed upon the army and people in general, that I began to have hopes of getting my liberty in a short time. I took all possible means of increasing this favourable opinion. The natives became, by degrees, less frightened of receiving any harm from me. Sometimes I would lie down and let five or six of them dance on my head. In the end the boys and girls would venture to come and play at hide-and-seek in my hair.

I had now made good progress in understanding and speaking their language. The Emperor had a mind one day to entertain me with several of the country shows, in which this people excelled all nations I have known, both for skill and splendour. I was diverted with none so much as that of the rope dancers. They performed upon a slender white thread stretched out for about two feet, and twelve inches from the ground. This rope dancing I desire permission, with the reader's patience, to describe at greater length.

This art is only practised by those persons, who wish for high offices and great favour at Court. They are trained in this art from their youth, and are not always of noble birth or a good education. When a great office is vacant, either by death or disgrace (which often happens), five or six of those who desire the office ask the Emperor to allow them to entertain His Majesty and the Court with a dance on the rope. Whoever jumps the highest, without falling, succeeds in getting the office. Very often the chief ministers are commanded to perform, and to let the Emperor see that they have not lost their skill.

The treasurer of the kingdom is allowed to cut a caper on the straight rope, at least an inch higher than any other lord in the whole empire. I have seen the officers turn a somersault several times together upon a plate fixed on a rope, which is no thicker than a common pack thread in England. The chief secretary for private affairs is in my opinion a good second to the treasurer. The rest of the great officers are all nearly equal.

These games are often attended by fatal accidents, of which there are a great number on record. I myself have seen two or three of the performers break their limbs. But the danger is much greater when the ministers themselves are commanded to show their skill. For, by striving to excel themselves and their fellows, they strain so far that there is hardly one of them who has not received a fall, and some of them two or three. I was told that, a year or two before my arrival, the treasurer would certainly have broken his neck if one of the Emperor's cushions, that by chance lay on the ground, had not weakened the force of his fall.

There is likewise another sport, which is only shown before the Emperor and the Empress, and the first minister, upon special occasions. The Emperor lays on the ground three fine silken threads six inches long, of which one is blue, the second red, and the third green. These threads are to be given as prizes to those persons whom the Emperor desires to distinguish by a special mark of his favour.

This sport is performed in His Majesty's great chamber of state, where the performers have to undergo a trial of skill very different from that of dancing on a rope. The like of it I have not seen in any other country of the new or old world. The Emperor holds a stick in his hands, while the performers, advancing one by one, sometimes leap over the stick, sometimes creep under it, backward and forward, several times, according as the stick is raised or lowered.

Sometimes the Emperor holds one end of the stick and his first minister the other; sometimes the minister has it entirely to himself. Whoever performs his part with the greatest skill is rewarded with the blue-coloured silk. The red is given to the next, and the green to the third, which they all wear girt twice round the waist. You see few persons about this Court who are not adorned with one of these girdles.

The horses of the army and those of the royal stables, having been daily led before me, were no longer shy, but would come to my very feet without starting. The riders would make them leap over my hand as I held it on the ground. One day one of the Emperor's huntsmen, upon a courser, made a great leap over my foot, shoe and all.

I had the good fortune to amuse the Emperor one day in a strange way. I wished him to order several sticks, two feet high, and as thick as an ordinary cane, to be brought to me. His Majesty at once gave commands to the master of his woods ·to get them, and the next morning six

woodmen arrived with six carriages, each drawn
by eight horses. I took nine of these sticks and
fixed them firmly in the ground in a four-sided
figure, two feet and a half square. I took four
other sticks, and tied them parallel at each corner,
about two feet from the ground.

Then I fastened my handkerchief to the nine
sticks that stood erect, and extended it on all sides
till it was tight as the top of a drum. The four
parallel sticks, rising about five inches higher
than the handkerchief, served as ledges on each
side. When I had finished, I requested the
Emperor to let a troop of his horses, twenty-four
in number, come and exercise upon this plain.

His Majesty approved of the proposal, and I
took them up, one by one, in my hands, ready
mounted and armed, with the proper officers to
exercise them. As soon as they got into order,
they divided into parties and performed sham
skirmishes. They discharged blunt arrows, drew
their swords, fled and pursued, attacked and
retired, and in short showed the best military
order I had ever seen.

The parallel sticks secured them and their
horses from falling over the stage. The Emperor
was so much delighted that he ordered this
entertainment to be repeated several days, and
once was pleased to be lifted up himself, and give

the word of command. With great difficulty he persuaded even the Empress herself to let me hold her in her chair within two yards of the stage, when she was able to get a fine view of the whole performance.

It was my good fortune that no accident happened at these entertainments. Only once, a fiery horse that belonged to one of the captains, pawing with his hoof, struck a hole in my handkerchief, and, his foot slipping, he overthrew himself and his rider. But I immediately freed them both, and covering the hole with one hand I set down the troop with the other, in the same way as I took them up. The horse that fell was strained in the left shoulder, but the rider got no hurt. I repaired my handkerchief as well as I could, but I would not trust the strength of it any more in such dangerous performances.

About two or three days before I was set at liberty, as I was entertaining the Court with feats of this kind, there arrived a messenger to inform His Majesty, that some of his subjects, while riding near the place where I was first taken, had seen a great black substance lying on the ground. This substance was very oddly shaped, with its edges extending round, as wide as His Majesty's bedroom, and rising up in the middle as high as a man.

They said that it was not a living creature, as they at first feared, for it lay on the grass without moving, and some of them had walked round it several times. They pointed out that, by mounting upon each other's shoulders, they had got to the top, which was flat and even, and that they had stamped upon it and found that it was hollow within. They thought that it might be something belonging to the Man-Mountain. If it pleased His Majesty, they would undertake to bring it with only five horses.

I soon knew what they meant, and was very glad to receive the news. It seems, upon my reaching the shore after our shipwreck, I was in such confusion that, before I came to the place where I went to sleep, my hat fell off after I came to land. I had fastened it on with a string to my head, while I was rowing, and it had stuck on all the time I was swimming. The string had been broken by some accident, though I thought I had lost it in the sea, for I never saw it when I came ashore.

I entreated His Majesty to give orders that it might be brought to me as soon as possible, and described to him its use and nature. The next day the wagoners arrived with it, but not in a very good condition. They had bored two holes in the brim, within an inch and a half of the edge, and

fastened two hooks in the holes. These hooks
were tied by a long cord to the harness, and in
this way my hat was dragged along for about a
mile. But, the ground in that country being very
smooth, it received less damage than I expected.

Two days after this adventure, the Emperor,
having ordered that part of his army which
quarters in and about his capital to be in readiness,
took a fancy to amusing himself in a very strange
way. He wished me to stand with my legs as far
asunder as I could. He then commanded his
general (who was an old, well-trained leader, and
a great friend of mine) to draw up the troops in
close order and march them under me, the foot
soldiers twenty-four abreast, and the horse sixteen
abreast, with drums beating, colours flying and
pikes advanced. This body consisted of three
thousand foot soldiers and a thousand horsemen.

I had sent so many letters asking for my liberty
that His Majesty at length mentioned the matter,
first in the cabinet and then in the full council.
It was opposed by the admiral of the kingdom,
who was pleased to be my mortal enemy, for no
reason that I knew of. But it was carried against
him by the whole council and confirmed by the
Emperor. However, this minister was at length
persuaded to agree, but did so on condition that
he himself was allowed to draw up the conditions

upon which I should be set free, and to which I must swear. These conditions were brought to me by the minister in person, attended by several persons of distinction.

After they were read I was demanded to swear that I would observe them, first in the manner of my own country, and afterwards in the method prescribed by their laws. This latter method was to hold my right foot in my left hand, and to place the middle finger of my right hand on the crown of my head, and my thumb on the tip of my right ear.

But because the reader may be curious to have some idea of the conditions on which I recovered my liberty, I give them here below:

'I. The Man-Mountain shall not depart from our dominions without permission under our great seal.

'II. He shall not presume to come into our metropolis, without our express order; at which time, the inhabitants shall have two hours' warning to keep within doors.

'III. The said Man-Mountain shall confine his walks to our principal highroads, and not offer to walk, or lie down, in a meadow or field of corn.

'IV. As he walks the said roads he shall take the utmost care not to trample upon the bodies of any of our loving subjects, their horses or their carriages, or take any of our subjects into his hands without their own consent.

'V. If an express requires great haste, the Man-Mountain shall be obliged to carry, in his pocket, the messenger and horse a six days' journey, once in every month, and return the said messenger (if so required) safe to our imperial presence.

'VI. He shall be our ally against our enemies in the island of Blefuscu, and do his utmost to destroy their fleet, which is now preparing to invade us.

'VII. That the said Man-Mountain shall, at his time of leisure, aid and assist our workmen, in helping to raise certain great stones, towards covering the wall of the principal park, and of our other royal buildings.

'VIII. That the said Man-Mountain shall, in two months' time deliver an exact survey of the circumference of our dominions, by counting the number of his own paces round the coast.

'Lastly. That, upon his solemn oath to observe all the above articles, the said Man-Mountain shall have a daily allowance of meat and drink, sufficient for the support of 1728 of our subjects, with free access to our royal person, and other marks of our favour. Given at our palace at Belfaborac, the twelfth day of the ninety-first month of our reign.'

I agreed to these conditions with great cheerfulness and content, although some of them were not so honourable as I could have wished. This proceeded wholly from the malice of the high-admiral. Upon this my chains were immediately unlocked, and I was at full liberty. The Emperor himself, in person, did me the honour to be present at the whole ceremony.

I made my acknowledgements by prostrating myself at His Majesty's feet. But he commanded me to rise. After many gracious expressions he added that he hoped I should prove a useful servant, and well deserve all the favours he had already given or might give me in the future.

4   THE CHIEF CITY OF LILLIPUT

The first request I made, after I had obtained my liberty, was, that I might have permission to see Mildendo, the metropolis. This the Emperor easily granted me, but with a special charge to do no hurt either to the inhabitants or their houses. The people had notice of my design to visit the town. The wall which runs round it is two feet and a half high, and at least eleven inches broad, so that a coach and horses may be driven safely round it. It is flanked with towers at ten feet distance.

I stepped over the great western gate, and passed very gently and sideways through the two principal streets in my short waistcoat only, for fear of damaging the roofs and eaves of the houses with the skirts of my coat. I walked with the utmost care, to avoid treading on any stragglers who might remain in the streets, although the orders were very strict, that all people should keep in their houses, at their own peril. The garret windows and tops of houses were so crowded with spectators that I thought in all my travels I had not seen a more populous place.

The city is an exact square, each side of the wall being five hundred feet long. The two great streets, which run across and divide it into four quarters, are five feet wide. The lanes and alleys, which I could not enter, but only view as I passed, are from twelve to eighteen inches wide. The town is capable of holding five hundred thousand souls. The houses are from three to five stories, and the shops and markets well provided.

The Emperor's palace is in the centre of the city, where the two great streets meet. It is enclosed by a wall two feet high, and twenty feet distant from the building. I had His Majesty's permission to step over this wall. The space

being so wide between that and the palace, I
could easily view it on every side. The outward
court is a square of forty feet, and includes two
other courts. In the inmost are the royal apartments, which I was very desirous of seeing, but
found it very difficult for the great gates, from
one square into another, were but eighteen inches
high, and seven inches wide.

Now the buildings of the outer court were at
least five feet high, and it was impossible for me
to stride over them without great damage to the
pile, though the walls were strongly built of
hewn stone, and four inches thick. At the same
time, the Emperor had a great desire that I should
see the splendours of his palace. But this I was not
able to do till three days after. This time I spent
in cutting down, with my knife, some of the
largest trees in the royal park, about a hundred
yards distant from the city.

Of these trees I made two stools, each about
three feet high, and strong enough to bear my
weight. The people having received notice a
second time, I went again through the city to the
palace, with my two stools in my hands. When I
came to the side of the outer court, I stood upon
one stool, and took the other in my hand. This I
lifted over the roof, and gently set it down on the
space between the first and second court, which

was eight feet wide. I then stepped over the
building from one stool to the other, and drew
up the first after me with a hooked stick.

By this means I got into the inner court.
Lying down upon my side, I put my face to the
windows of the middle stories, which were left
open on purpose, and saw the most splendid

apartments that could be imagined. There I saw the Empress and the young princes, in their several rooms, with their chief attendants about them. Her Majesty was pleased to smile very graciously upon me, and gave me out of the window her hand to kiss.

One morning, about a fortnight after I had obtained my liberty, the secretary for private affairs came to my house, attended only by one servant. He ordered his coach to wait at a distance, and desired I would give him an hour's audience. This I readily consented to, on account of his quality and personal merits, as well as of the many good offices he had done me at Court. I offered to lie down, that he might reach my ear. But he chose rather to let me hold him in my hand during our conversation.

He began with compliments on my liberty, and said he might pretend to some merit in it. But he added that if it had not been for the present situation of things at Court, perhaps I might not have obtained it so soon. 'For,' said he, 'as flourishing a condition as we may appear to be in, to foreigners, we labour under two mighty evils; a violent faction at home, and the danger of an invasion by a most powerful enemy from abroad. As to the first, you are to understand that for about seventy months past there have been two struggling parties in this empire, under the name of "High Heels" and "Low Heels".

'It is said, indeed, that the high heels are most agreeable to our ancient laws. But, however this may be, His Majesty has determined to make use only of low heels in the work of his government, and in all offices in the gift of the Crown, as you cannot but observe. His Majesty's heels are lower by at least a *drurr* than any of his Court (*drurr* is a measure about the fourteenth part of an inch). The hatred between these two parties runs so high that they will neither eat, nor drink, nor talk with each other. We reckon that High Heels exceed us in number, but the power is wholly on our side.

'We are afraid that His Highness, the heir to the crown, has some tendency towards the High Heels. At least we can plainly see that one of his heels is higher than the other, which gives him a hobble in his walk. Now, in the midst of these quarrels at home, we are threatened with an invasion from the island of Blefuscu, which is the other great empire of the world, almost as large and powerful as this of His Majesty.

'For as to what we have heard you affirm, that there are other kingdoms and states in the world inhabited by human creatures as large as yourself, our wise men are in much doubt, and would rather believe that you dropped from the moon

or one of the stars. It is certain that a hundred
mortals of your size would in a short time destroy
all the fruits and cattle of His Majesty's dominions.
And our histories of six thousand months make
no mention of any other regions than those of the
two great empires of Lilliput and Blefuscu.

'These two mighty powers have, as I was going
to tell you, been engaged in a most stubborn war
for six-and-thirty months past. It began upon the
following occasion. It is allowed on all hands that
the first way of breaking eggs, before we eat them,
was upon the larger end. But His Majesty's
grandfather, while he was a boy, going to eat an
egg, and breaking it according to the ancient
practice, happened to cut one of his fingers. On
this the Emperor, his father, passed a law, com-
manding all his subjects, upon great penalties, to
break the smaller ends of their eggs.

'The people so greatly objected to this law that,
our histories tell us, there have been six rebellions
raised on that account. In one of these one
Emperor lost his life, and another his crown.
These civil wars were constantly fanned by the
monarchs of Blefuscu. When they were quelled,
the exiles always fled for refuge to that empire. It
is reckoned that eleven thousand persons have
suffered death rather than submit to break their
eggs at the smaller ends.

'Now, the Big-endian exiles have found so much credit in the Emperor of Blefuscu's Court, and so much private assistance and encouragement from their private party here at home, that a bitter war has been carried on between the two empires for six-and-thirty months, with varied success. During this time we have lost forty large ships, and a much greater number of smaller vessels, together with thirty thousand of our best seamen and soldiers. The damage received by the enemy is reckoned to be somewhat greater than ours.

'However, they have now equipped a numerous fleet, and are just preparing to make a descent upon us. His Majesty, placing great confidence in your valour and strength, has commanded me to lay this account of his affairs before you.'

I desired the secretary to present my humble duty to the Emperor, and to let him know that I thought it would not become me, who was a foreigner, to interfere with parties. But I was ready, at the risk of my life, to defend his person and State against all invaders.

5   HOW GULLIVER CAPTURED
A WHOLE FLEET

The empire of Blefuscu is an island situated to
the north-east of Lilliput, from which it is parted
only by a channel eight hundred yards wide. I had
not yet seen it, and upon this notice of an intended invasion I avoided appearing on that side
of the coast, for fear of being seen by some of the
enemy's ships, who had received no news of me.
All intercourse between the two empires having
been strictly forbidden during the war, upon pain
of death, none of the Emperor's vessels were
allowed to go there.

I told His Majesty of a project I had formed, of
seizing the enemy's whole fleet. The fleet, as our
scouts assured us, lay at anchor in the harbour,
ready to sail with the first fair wind. I consulted
the most experienced seamen about the depth of
the channel, which they had often sounded. They
told me that in the middle, at high water, it was
seventy *glumgluffs* deep, which is about six feet of
European measure; and the rest of it fifty *glumgluffs* at most.

I walked towards the north-east coast, over
against Blefuscu. There, lying down behind a
hillock, I took out my small glass, and viewed the

enemy's fleet at anchor, consisting of about fifty men-of-war, and a great number of transports. I then came back to my house, and gave orders for a great quantity of the strongest cable and bars of iron. The cable was about as thick as pack-thread, and the bars of the length and size of a knitting-needle.

I trebled the cable to make it stronger, and for the same reason I twisted three of the iron bars together, bending the ends into a hook. Having thus fixed fifty hooks to as many cables, I went back to the north-east coast, and, putting off my coat, shoes, and stockings, walked into the sea in my leathern jerkin, about half an hour before high water. I waded with what haste I could, and swam in the middle about thirty yards, till I felt ground. I arrived at the fleet in less than half an hour.

The enemy were so frightened when they saw me that they leaped out of their ships and swam to shore, where there could not be fewer than thirty thousand souls. I then took my tackling, and fastening a hook to the hole at the prow of each, I tied all the cords together at the end. While I was thus employed, the enemy discharged several thousand arrows, many of which stuck in my hands and face. Besides the great smart they caused, they gave me much disturbance in my work. My greatest fear was for my eyes, which I should have lost, if I had not suddenly thought of a plan for saving them.

I kept, among other little needful things, a pair of glasses, in a private pocket, which, as I observed before, had escaped the Emperor's searchers. These I took out, and fastened as firmly as I could upon my nose, and, thus armed, went on boldly with my work, in spite of the enemy's arrows. Many of them struck against the glasses of my spectacles, but without any other effect than to disarrange them a little.

I had now fastened all the hooks, and, taking the knot in my hand, I began to pull. But not a ship would stir, for they were all held too fast by their anchors. So that the boldest part of my plan remained. I therefore let go the cord, and, leaving the hooks fixed to the ships, I cut with my knife the cables that fastened the anchors. While doing so I received about two hundred shots in my face and hands. Then I took up the knotted end of the cables, to which my hooks were tied, and with the greatest ease drew fifty of the enemy's largest men-of-war after me.

The Blefuscudians, who had not the least thought of what I intended, were at first taken by surprise. They had seen me cut the cables, and thought my design was only to let the ships run

adrift, or fall foul of each other. But when they perceived the whole fleet moving in order, and saw me pulling at the end, they set up such a scream of grief and despair as it is almost impossible to describe or think of.

When I had got out of danger, I stopped awhile to pick out the arrows that had stuck in my hands and face. I now rubbed on some of the same ointment that was given me on my first arrival, as I have formerly mentioned. I then took off my glasses, and waiting about an hour, till the tide was a little lower, I waded through the middle with my cargo, and arrived safe at the royal port of Lilliput.

The Emperor and his whole Court stood on the shore, awaiting the result of this great adventure. They saw the ships move forward in a large half-moon, but could not see me, who was up to my breast in water. When I advanced to the middle of the channel, they were yet in pain, because I was under water to my neck. The Emperor concluded that I was drowned, and that the enemy's fleet was approaching to fight. But he was soon relieved of his fears, for, the channel growing shallower every step I made, I came in a short time within hearing, and holding up the end of the cable, by which the fleet was fastened, I cried in a loud voice: 'Long live the powerful king of Lilliput!' This great prince received me at my landing with all possible joy, and created me a *nardac* upon the spot, which is the highest title of honour among them.

His Majesty desired I would take some other opportunity of bringing all the rest of his enemy's ships into his ports. And so great is the ambition of princes that he seemed to think of nothing less than reducing the whole empire of Blefuscu into a province, and governing it by a viceroy. He wished to destroy the Big-endian exiles, and compel that people to break the smaller ends of their eggs, by which he would remain the sole monarch of the world.

But I tried to divert him from this design, and I plainly protested that I would never be the agent to bring a free and brave people into slavery; and, when the matter was debated in council, the wisest part of the ministry were of my opinion.

This open, bold declaration of mine was so much against the schemes and politics of His Majesty that he could never forgive me. He mentioned it in a very artful manner at council, where I was told that some of the wisest appeared at least, by their silence, to be of my opinion. But others, who were my enemies, could not forbear some expressions which by a side wind reflected on me. From this time began a plotting between His Majesty and a number of ministers, bent against me, which broke out in less than two months, and appeared likely to end in my utter destruction. Of so little weight are the greatest services to princes, when put into the balance with a refusal to gratify their passions.

About three weeks after this adventure, there arrived a solemn embassy from Blefuscu, with humble offers of a peace. This was soon concluded upon conditions very advantageous to our Emperor, wherewith I shall not trouble the reader. There were six ambassadors, with a train of about five hundred persons. Their entry was very magnificent, suitable to the grandeur of their master and the importance of their business.

When their treaty was finished, in connection with which I did them several good offices by the credit I now had, or at least appeared to have, at Court, their excellencies, who were privately told how much I had been their friend, made me a visit in form. They began with many compliments upon my valour and kindness, invited me to that kingdom, in the Emperor their master's name, and desired me to show them some proofs of my huge strength, of which they had heard so many wonders. I readily obliged them in this, but shall not trouble the reader with the particulars.

When I had for some time entertained their excellencies, to their great satisfaction and surprise, I desired they would do me the honour to present my most humble respects to the Emperor their master, the renown of whose virtues had so justly filled the whole world with admiration, and whose royal person I resolved to visit, before I returned to my own country.

Accordingly, the next time I had the honour to see the Emperor, I desired his general permission to wait on the Blefuscudian monarch, which he was pleased to grant me, as I could perceive, in a very cold manner. But I could not guess the reason, till I had a whsiper from a certain person that the high treasurer and the high admiral had represented my intercourse with those ambassadors as a mark of disaffection. From this I am sure my heart was wholly free. And this was the first time I began to conceive some imperfect idea of Courts and ministers.

It is to be observed that these ambassadors spoke to me by an interpreter, the languages of both empires differing as much from each other as any two in Europe, and each nation priding itself upon the age, beauty, and energy of its own tongue, with an avowed contempt of that of its neighbour. Yet our Emperor, standing upon the advantage he had got by the seizure of their fleet, obliged them to make their speech in the Lilliputian tongue.

And it must be confessed, that from the great intercourse of trade and commerce between both kingdoms, and from the custom, in each empire, to send its young nobles and richer gentry to the other, in order to polish themselves by seeing the world, and understanding men and manners, there are few persons of distinction, or merchants, or seamen, who dwell in the coast parts, but can hold conversation in both tongues. I found this out some weeks after, when I went to pay my respects to the Emperor of Blefuscu, which in the midst of great misfortunes through the malice of my enemies, proved a very happy adventure to me, as I shall relate in its proper place.

6   GULLIVER LEAVES LILLIPUT

Before I proceed to give an account of my leaving this kingdom, it may be proper to inform the reader of a private plot, which had been for two months forming against me.

I had been hitherto, all my life, a stranger to Courts, for which I was unqualified by the meanness of my condition. I had, indeed, heard and read enough of the natures of great princes and ministers, but I never expected to have found such terrible effects of them in so remote a country, governed, as I thought, by very different rules from those in Europe.

While I was just preparing to visit the Emperor of Blefuscu, an important person at Court (to whom I had rendered great service at a time when he lay under the highest displeasure of His Majesty) came to my house very privately at night in a close chair, and, without sending in his name, desired admittance.

The chair-bearers were dismissed, and I put the chair, with his lordship in it, into my coat pocket. I then gave orders to a trusty servant to say I was ill and gone to sleep. I fastened the door of my house, placed the chair on the table, according to my usual custom, and sat down by it. His lordship's face was full of concern, and on my inquiring into the reason he informed me that His Majesty and council had condemned me to the loss of my eyes, as I had been found guilty of treason. In three days the secretary would be directed to come to my house, and would read the resolution come to with regard to me.

After thinking over the matter for some time, I fixed upon a plan, for which it is possible I may incur some blame, and not unjustly. I confess I owe the preserving of my eyes, and as a result of my liberty, to my own great rashness and want of experience. If I had then known the nature of princes and ministers, which I have since observed in many other Courts, and their methods of treating greater criminals than myself, I should have submitted with great readiness to so easy a punishment.

But hurried on by the rashness of youth, and having His Majesty's permission to visit the Emperor of Blefuscu, I took the chance, before the three days were passed, to send a letter to my friend the secretary, telling him that I had resolved to set out that morning for Blefuscu.

Without waiting for an answer I went to that side of the island where our fleet lay. I seized a large man-of-war, and tied the cable to the prow. Lifting up the anchors, I stripped myself, put my clothes (together with my coverlet, which I carried under my arm) into the vessel, and, drawing it after me, between wading and swimming I arrived at the royal port of Blefuscu, where the people had long expected me.

They lent me two guides to direct me to the capital city, which is of the same name. I held them in my hands till I came within two hundred yards of the gate, and desired them to tell of my arrival to one of the secretaries, and let him know I there waited His Majesty's commands. I had an answer in about an hour, that His Majesty, attended by the royal family and great officers of the Court, was coming out to receive me. I advanced a hundred yards.

The Emperor and his train alighted from their horses, the Empress and ladies from their coaches, and I did not perceive they were in any fright or concern. I lay on the ground to kiss His Majesty's and the Empress's hands. I told His Majesty that I was come according to my promise, and with the permission of the Emperor my master, to have the honour of seeing so mighty a monarch, and to offer him any service in my power, as far as my duty to my own prince would allow. I did not mention a word of my disgrace, because I had hitherto no regular information of it, and might suppose myself wholly ignorant of any such design. I could not reasonably conceive that the Emperor would find out the secret, while I was out of his power. In this, however, it soon appeared I was deceived.

I shall not trouble the reader with the account of my reception at this Court, which was suitable to the kindness of so great a prince. Nor shall I say anything of the difficulties I was in for want of a house and bed, being forced to lie on the ground, wrapped up in my coverlet.

Three days after my arrival, walking, out of

curiosity, to the north-east coast of the island, I observed, about half a league off in the sea, something that looked like a boat overturned. I pulled off my shoes and stockings, and, wading two or three hundred yards, I found the object to approach nearer by the force of the tide. Then I plainly saw it to be a real boat, which I supposed might by some tempest have been driven from a ship. Upon this I returned immediately towards the city, and desired His Majesty to lend me twenty of the tallest vessels he had left, after the loss of his fleet, and three thousand seamen, under the command of his vice-admiral.

This fleet sailed round while I went back the shortest way to the coast, where I first saw the boat. I found the tide had driven it still nearer. The seamen were all provided with cords, which I had beforehand twisted to a sufficient strength. When the ships came up, I stripped myself, and waded till I came within a hundred yards of the boat, after which I was forced to swim till I got up to it.

The seamen threw me the end of the cord, which I fastened to a hole in the forepart of the boat, and the other end to a man-of-war. But I found all my labour to little purpose; for, being out of my depth, I was not able to work. In this necessity I was forced to swim behind, and push the boat forward, as often as I could, with one of my hands. The tide favouring me, I advanced so far that I could just hold up my chin and feel the ground. I rested two or three minutes, and then gave the boat another shove, and so on, till the sea was no higher than my armpits.

The hardest part being now over, I took out my other cables, which were stowed in one of the ships, and fastened them first to the boat and then to nine of the vessels which attended me. The wind being favourable, the seamen towed and I shoved, until we arrived within forty yards of the shore, and, waiting till the tide was out, I got to the boat dry. By the help of two thousand men, with ropes and engines, I made a shift to turn it on its bottom, and found it was but little damaged.

I shall not trouble the reader with the difficulties I was under, by the help of certain paddles, which cost me ten days making, to get my boat into the royal port of Blefuscu. A mighty crowd of people appeared upon my arrival, full of wonder at the sight of so large a vessel. I told the Emperor that my good fortune had thrown this boat in my way to carry me to some place whence I might return to my native country; and begged His Majesty's orders for getting things to fit it up, together with his permission to depart. After some trouble, he was pleased to grant this.

I did very much wonder, in all this time, not to have heard of any message relating to me being sent from our Emperor to the Court of Blefuscu. But I was afterwards given privately to understand, that his Majesty, never thinking I had the least notice of his designs, believed I was only gone to Blefuscu according to my promise and the permission he had given me, which was well known at our Court, and would return in a few days, when the ceremony was ended.

But he was at last in pain at my long absence. After consulting with the treasurer and the rest of my enemies, a person of quality was sent with a copy of the articles against me. This envoy had instructions to represent to the monarch of Blefuscu the great kindness of his master, who was content to punish me no further than the loss of mine eyes; that I had fled from justice; and if I did not return in two hours, I should be deprived of my title of *nardac*, and declared a traitor. The envoy further added, that in order to maintain the peace and amity between both empires, his master expected that his brother of Blefuscu would give orders to have me sent back to Lilliput, bound hand and foot, to be punished as a traitor.

The Emperor of Blefuscu, having taken three days to consult, returned an answer consisting of many civilities and excuses. He said that, as for sending me bound, his brother knew it was impossible; that although I had taken away his fleet, yet he owed great thanks to me for many good offices I had done him in making the peace. However, both their majesties would soon be made easy. For I had found a huge vessel on the shore, able to carry me on the sea, which he had given orders to fit up with my own help and direction. He hoped in a few weeks both empires would be freed from my presence.

With this answer the envoy returned to Lilliput, and the monarch of Blefuscu related to me all that had passed. He offered me at the same time (but under the strictest confidence) his gracious protection, if I would continue in his service. Although I believed him sincere, yet I resolved never more to put any confidence in princes or ministers, where I could possibly avoid it. Therefore, with all due acknowledgement of his kindly intentions, I humbly begged to be excused. I told him that, since fortune, whether good or evil, had thrown a vessel in my way, I was resolved to venture myself on the ocean, rather than be a cause of difference between two such mighty monarchs. I did not find the Emperor at all displeased, and I found, by a certain accident, that he was very glad of my resolve, and so were most of his ministers.

These reasons moved me to hasten my departure somewhat sooner than I intended. The Court, impatient to have me gone, very readily helped in my plan. Five hundred workmen were employed to make two sails to my boat according to my directions, by quilting thirteen folds of their strongest linen together. I was at the pains of making ropes and cables, by twisting ten, twenty, or thirty of the thickest and strongest of theirs.

A great stone that I happened to find, after a long search by the seashore, served me for an anchor. I had the tallow of three hundred cows for greasing my boat, and other uses. I was at great pains in cutting down some of the largest timber trees for oars and masts. In this I was, however, much assisted by His Majesty's ship-carpenters, who helped me in smoothing them, after I had done the rough work.

In about a month, when all was prepared, I sent to receive His Majesty's commands, and to take my leave. The Emperor and royal family came out of the palace. I lay down on my face to kiss his hand, which he very graciously gave me. So did the Empress and the young princes of the blood. His Majesty presented me with fifty purses of two hundred *sprugs* a-piece, together with his picture at full length, which I put immediately into one of my gloves, to keep it from being hurt. The ceremonies at my departure were too many to trouble the reader with at this time.

I stored the boat with the carcasses of a hundred oxen and three hundred sheep, with some bread and drink, and as much meat ready dressed as four hundred cooks could provide. I took with me six cows and two bulls alive, with as many ewes and rams, intending to carry them into my own country. To feed them on board, I had a good bundle of hay, and a bag of corn.

I would gladly have taken a dozen of the natives, but this was a thing the Emperor would by no means permit. Besides a diligent search into my pockets, His Majesty engaged my honour not to carry away any of his subjects, unless with their own consent and desire.

Having thus prepared all things as well as I was able, I set sail on the twenty-fourth day of September, 1701, at six in the morning. When I had gone about four leagues to the northward, the wind being at the south-east, at six in the evening I saw a small island, about half a league to the north-west. I advanced forward, and cast anchor on the lee side of the island, which seemed to be uninhabited.

I then took some food, and went to my rest. I slept well, as I believe for at least six hours, for I found the day broke in two hours after I awoke. It was a clear night. I ate my breakfast before the sun was up. Heaving anchor, the wind being favourable, I then steered the same course that I had done the day before, as I was directed by my pocket compass. My intention was to reach, if possible, one of those islands which I had reason to believe lay to the north-east of Van Diemen's Land.

I found nothing all that day; but upon the next, about three in the afternoon, when I had by my reckoning made twenty-four leagues from Blefuscu, I saw a sail steering to the south-east. My course was due east. I hailed her, but could get no answer. Yet I found that I gained upon her, for the wind slackened. I made all the sail I could, and in half an hour she spied me, and fired a gun. It is not easy to express the joy I was in, upon the unexpected hope of once more seeing my beloved country, and the dear pledges I left in it.

The ship slackened her sails, and I came up with her between five and six in the evening, September 26. My heart leaped within me to see her English colours. I put my cows and sheep into my coat pocket, and got on board with all my little cargo of provisions.

I shall not trouble the reader with a particular account of this voyage, which was very prosperous for the most part. We arrived in the Downs on the 13th of April, 1702.

A VOYAGE TO BROBDINGNAG

(H 757)

ꜱ A Voyage to Brobdingnag ꜱ

I HOW GULLIVER FELL INTO STRANGE
COMPANY

Having been condemned, by nature and fortune, to an active and restless life, in two months after my return I again left my native country on the good ship *Adventure*, bound for Surat. We had a very prosperous voyage, till we arrived at the Cape of Good Hope, where we landed for fresh water. But discovering a leak, we unshipped our goods, and wintered there. The captain fell ill, and we could not leave the Cape till the end of March.

We then set sail, and had a good voyage till we passed the Straits of Madagascar. But having got northward of that island, and to about five degrees south latitude, the winds, which in those seas are observed to blow a constant equal gale between the north and west, from the beginning of December to the beginning of May, began on the 19th of April to blow with much greater violence, and more westerly than usual, continuing so for twenty days together.

During this storm, which was followed by a
strong wind west-south-west, we were carried,
by my reckoning, about five hundred leagues to
the east, so that the oldest sailor on board could
not tell in what part of the world we were.

On the 16th day of June, 1703, a boy on the
topmast discovered land. When we came to it, we
saw no river or spring, or any sign of inhabitants.
Our men therefore wandered on the shore to
find out some fresh water near the sea, and I
walked alone about a mile on the other side,
where I observed the country all barren and rocky.
I now began to be weary, and, seeing nothing to
entertain my curiosity, I returned slowly down
towards the creek. The sea being full in my view,
I saw our men already got into the boat, and
rowing for life to the ship.

I was going to shout after them, although it
had been to little purpose, when I observed a
huge creature walking after them in the sea, as
fast as he could. He waded not much deeper than
his knees, and took great strides. But our men
had the start of him half a league, and, the sea
thereabouts being full of sharp-pointed rocks, the
monster was not able to overtake the boat.

This I was afterwards told, for I durst not stay
to see the result of the adventure. But I ran as
fast as I could the way I first went, and then

climbed up a steep hill, that gave me a view of the country. I found it fully cultivated. But that which first surprised me was the length of the grass, which, in those grounds that seemed to be kept for hay, was about twenty feet high.

I fell into a highroad, for so I took it to be, though it served to the inhabitants only as a footpath, through a field of barley. Here I walked on for some time, but could see little on either side, it being now near harvest, and the corn rising at least forty feet. I was an hour walking to the end of this field, which was fenced in with a hedge of at least one hundred and twenty feet high, and the trees so lofty that I could not tell their height.

There was a stile to pass from this field into the next. It had four steps, and a stone to cross over when you came to the uppermost. It was impossible for me to climb this stile, because every step was six feet high, and the upper stone about twenty. I was trying to find some gap in the hedge, when I found one of the inhabitants in the next field, advancing towards the stile, of the same size with him whom I saw in the sea pursuing our boat.

He appeared as tall as a church spire, and took about ten yards at every stride, as near as I could guess. I was struck with the utmost fear and astonishment, and ran to hide myself in the corn. From my hiding place I saw him at the top of the stile looking back into the next field on the right hand, and heard him call in a voice many degrees louder than a speaking trumpet. But the noise was so high in the air, that at first I certainly thought it was thunder. Upon this seven monsters, like himself, came towards him, with reaping hooks in their hands, each hook about the size of six scythes.

These people were not so well clad as the first, whose servants or labourers they seemed to be, for, upon some words he spoke, they went to reap the corn where I lay. I kept from them at as great a distance as I could, but was forced to move with great difficulty, for the stalks of corn were sometimes not above a foot distant, so that I could hardly squeeze my body betwixt them. However, I made a shift to go forward, till I came to a part of the field where the corn had been laid by the rain and wind. Here it was impossible for me to advance a step, for the stalks were so interwoven that I could not creep through, and the beards of the fallen ears so strong and pointed that they pierced through my clothes into my flesh.

At the same time I heard the reapers not above a hundred yards behind me. Being quite tired with toil, and wholly overcome by grief and despair, I lay down between two ridges, and heartily wished I might there end my days. I bemoaned my lonely widow and fatherless children. I lamented my own folly and wilfulness, in attempting a second voyage, against the advice of all my friends and relations.

In this terrible state of mind, I could not forbear thinking of Lilliput, whose inhabitants looked upon me as the greatest wonder that ever appeared in the world, where I was able to draw a fleet in my hand, and perform those other actions, which will be recorded for ever in the chronicles of that empire. I reflected what a pity it must prove to me to appear as small in this nation as one single Lilliputian would be among us.

But this I thought was to be the least of my misfortunes; for, as human creatures are observed to be more savage and cruel in proportion to their size, what could I expect but to be a morsel in the mouth of the first among these huge barbarians who should happen to seize me?

Frightened as I was, I could not forbear going on with these thoughts, when one of the reapers, approaching within ten yards of the ridge where I lay, made me fear that with the next step I should be crushed to death under his foot, or cut in two with his reaping-hook. Therefore, when he

was again about to move, I screamed as loud as
fear could make me. Then the huge creature trod
short and, looking round about under him for some
time, at last espied me as I lay on the ground.

He considered awhile, with the caution of one
who tries to lay hold of a small dangerous animal
in such a manner that it shall not be able either to

scratch or bite him. At length he took me behind, by the middle, between his forefinger and thumb, and brought me within three yards of his eyes, that he might behold my shape more perfectly. I guessed his meaning, and my good fortune gave me so much presence of mind that I resolved not to struggle in the least as he held me in the air, above sixty feet from the ground, although he pinched my sides, for fear I should slip through his fingers.

All I did was to raise mine eyes towards the sun, and place my hands together, and to speak some words in a humble, sad tone, suitable to the condition I was then in. For I feared every moment that he would dash me against the ground, as we usually do any little hateful animal which we have a mind to destroy. But my good star would have it that he appeared pleased with my voice and gestures, and began to look upon me as a strange sight, much wondering to hear me speak some words, although he could not understand them.

In the meantime I was not able to forbear groaning and shedding tears, and turning my head towards my sides; letting him know, as well as I could, how cruelly I was hurt by the pressure of his thumb and finger. He seemed to understand my meaning, for, lifting up the lappet of his coat, he put me gently into it, and immediately ran along with me to his master, who was a farmer, and the same person I had first seen in the field.

The farmer having (as I supposed by their talk) received such an account of me as his servant could give him, took a piece of a small straw, about the size of a walking-staff, and therewith lifted up the lappets of my coat. This it seems he thought to be some kind of covering that nature had given me. He blew my hair aside to take a better view of my face. He called his hinds about him, and asked them, as I afterwards learned, whether they had ever seen any little creature in the fields that looked like me.

He then placed me softly on the ground upon all-fours, but I got immediately up, and walked slowly backward and forward, to let those people see I had no intention of running away. They all sat down in a circle about me, the better to observe my movements. I pulled off my hat, and made a low bow towards the farmer. I fell on my knees, and lifted up my hands and eyes, and spoke several words as loud as I could. I took a purse of gold out of my pocket, and humbly presented it to him.

He received it on the palm of his hand, then applied it close to his eye to see what it was, and afterwards turned it several times with the point of a pin (which he took out of his sleeve), but could make nothing of it. Whereupon I made a sign that he should place his hand on the ground. I then took the purse, and, opening it, poured all the gold into his palm. There were six Spanish pieces, beside twenty or thirty smaller coins. I saw him wet the tip of his little finger upon his tongue, and take up one of my largest pieces, and then another. But he did not seem to know what they were. He made me a sign to put them again into my purse, and the purse again into my pocket which, after offering it to him several times, I thought it best to do.

The farmer, by this time, was sure I must be a rational creature. He spoke often to me. But the sound of his voice pierced my ears like that of a water-mill, yet his words were clear enough. I answered as loud as I could in several languages, and he often laid his ear within two yards of me. But all in vain, for we did not understand each other.

He then sent his servants to their work, and taking his handkerchief out of his pocket, he doubled and spread it on his left hand. This he placed flat on the ground, with the palm upward, making me a sign to step into it, as I could easily do, for it was not above a foot in thickness. I thought it my part to obey, and, for fear of falling laid myself at full length upon the handkerchief, with the remainder of which he wrapped me up to the head for further safety. In this manner he carried me home to his house.

There he called his wife, and showed me to her. But she screamed and ran back, as women in England do at the sight of a toad or a spider. However, when she had seen my conduct, and how well I observed the signs her husband made, she was soon quite pleased, and by degrees grew very tender of me.

It was about twelve at noon, and a servant brought in dinner. It was only one dish of meat (fit for the plain condition of a husbandman), in a dish of about four-and-twenty feet diameter. The company were the farmer, and his wife, three children, and an old grandmother. When they had sat down, the farmer placed me at some distance from him on the table, which was thirty feet high from the floor.

I was in a terrible fright, and kept as far as I could from the edge, for fear of falling. The wife minced a bit of meat, then crumbled some bread on a trencher, and placed it before me. I made her a low bow, took out my knife and fork, and fell to eat, which gave them great delight. The mistress sent her maid for a small cup, which held about two gallons, and filled it with drink.

I took up the vessel with much difficulty in both hands, and in a most respectful manner drank to her ladyship's health, expressing the words as loud as I could in English, which made the company laugh so heartily that I was almost deafened with the noise. This drink tasted like a small cider, and was not unpleasant. Then the master made me a sign to come to the side of his trencher. But as I walked on the table, being in great surprise all the time, as the reader will easily think and excuse, I happened to stumble against a crust, and fell flat on my face, but received no hurt.

I got up immediately, and observing the good people to be in much concern, I took my hat (which I held under my arm out of good manners) and waving it over my head, made three huzzas, to show I had got no mischief by my fall. But, advancing forward towards my master (as I shall henceforth call him), his youngest son, who sat next to him, a boy of about ten years old, took me up by the legs, and held me so high in the air that I trembled in every limb. But his father snatched me from him, and at the same time gave him such a box on the left ear as would have felled a European troop of horse to the earth, and ordered him to be taken from the table.

Being afraid this boy might owe me a spite, and

well remembering how mischievous all children among us naturally are to sparrows, rabbits, young kittens, and puppy dogs, I fell on my knees, and, pointing to the boy, made my master understand as well as I could, that I desired his son might be pardoned. The father agreed, and the lad took his seat again, and I went to him and kissed his hand, which my master took, and made him stroke me gently with.

In the midst of dinner, my mistress's favourite cat leaped into her lap. I heard a noise behind me like that of a dozen stocking-weavers at work. Turning my head, I found it came from the purring of that animal, who seemed to be three times larger than an ox, as I thought by the view of her head, and one of her paws, while her mistress was feeding and stroking her.

The fierceness of this creature's face altogether frightened me, though I stood at the farther end of the table, above fifty feet off, and though my mistress held her fast, for fear she might give a spring, and seize me in her claws. But it happened there was no danger, for the cat took not the least notice of me, when my master placed me within three yards of her.

As I have been always told, and found true by experience in my travels, that flying or showing fear before a fierce animal is a certain way to make it pursue or attack you, so I resolved to show no manner of concern. I walked with courage five or six times before the very head of the cat, and came within half a yard of her. On this she drew herself back, as if she were afraid of me. I had less fear concerning the dogs, of which three or four came into the room, as it is usual in farmers' houses. One of them was a mastiff, equal in size to four elephants, and a greyhound, somewhat taller than the mastiff, but not so large.

When dinner was almost done, the nurse came in with a child of a year old in her arms, who immediately spied me, and began a squall that you might have heard from London Bridge to Chelsea, after the usual way of infants, to get me for a plaything. The mother took me up, and put me towards the child, who presently seized me by the middle, and put my head into his mouth. At this I roared so loudly that the urchin was frightened, and let me drop, and I should have broken my neck, if the mother had not held her apron under me. The nurse, to quieten her babe, made use of a rattle, which was a kind of hollow vessel filled with great stones, and fastened by a cable to the child's waist.

When dinner was done, my master went out to his labourers, and, as I could make out by his voice and gesture, gave his wife a strict charge to take care of me. I was very much tired, and disposed to sleep. My mistress, seeing this, put me on her own bed, and covered me with a clean white handkerchief, but larger and coarser than the mainsail of a man-of-war.

I slept about two hours, and dreamt I was at home with my wife and children, which increased my sorrows when I awoke, and found myself alone in a vast room, between two and three hundred feet wide, and about two hundred high, lying in a bed twenty yards wide. My mistress was gone about her household affairs, and had locked me in. The bed was eight yards from the floor. While I was in bed, two rats crept up the curtains, and ran smelling backwards and forwards on my bed.

One of them came up almost to my face, and I rose in a fright, and drew out my sword to defend myself. These horrible animals had the boldness to attack me on both sides, and one of them held his fore feet at my collar. But I had the good fortune to kill him before he could do me any mischief. He fell down at my feet, and the other, seeing the fate of his comrade, made his escape, but not without one good wound on the back, which I gave him as he fled, and made the blood run trickling from him.

After this deed, I walked gently to and fro on

the bed, to recover my breath and loss of spirits. These creatures were of the size of a large mastiff, but more nimble and fierce. So that if I had taken off my belt before I went to sleep, I must have been torn to pieces and devoured. I measured the tail of the dead rat, and found it to be two yards long, wanting an inch. But I did not like to draw

7   (H 757)

the carcass off the bed, where it lay still bleeding. I observed it had yet some life, but with a strong slash across the neck, I thoroughly killed it.

Soon after, my mistress came into the room, who, seeing me all covered with blood, ran and took me up in her hand. I pointed to the dead rat, smiling, and making other signs to show I was not hurt. At this she was greatly rejoiced, calling the maid to take up the dead rat with a pair of tongs and throw it out of the window. Then she set me on a table, where I showed her my sword all blood, and, wiping it on the lappet of my coat, returned it to the sheath.

2   GULLIVER MAKES THE FARMER'S FORTUNE

My mistress had a daughter of nine years old, a child of towardly parts for her age, very clever at her needle, and skilful in dressing her doll. Her mother and she fitted up the doll's cradle for me against night. The cradle was put into a small drawer of a cabinet, and the drawer placed upon a hanging shelf for fear of the rats. This was my bed all the time I stayed with those people, though made more convenient by degrees, as I began to learn their language, and make my wants known.

This young girl was my schoolmistress, to teach me the language. When I pointed to anything, she told me the name of it in her own tongue, so that in a few days I was able to call for whatever I had a mind to. She was very good-natured and not above forty feet high, being little for her age. She gave me the name of *Mannikin*. To her I chiefly owe my safety in that country; we never parted while I was there. I called her my *Glumdalclitch*, or little nurse. I should be very ungrateful, if I omitted this honourable mention of her care and affection towards me, which I heartily wish it lay in my power to requite as she deserves, instead of being the innocent but unhappy means of her disgrace, as I have too much reason to fear.

It now began to be known and talked of in the neighbourhood, that my master had found a strange animal in the field exactly shaped in every part like a human creature, which it likewise imitated in all its actions. It seemed to speak in a little language of its own, had already learned several words of theirs, went erect upon two legs, was tame and gentle, would come when it was called, do whatever it was bid, and had the finest limbs in the world, and a complexion fairer than a nobleman's daughter of three years old.

Another farmer, who lived hard by, and was a great friend of my master, came on a visit on purpose to inquire into the truth of this story. I was immediately produced, and placed upon a table, where I walked as I was commanded, drew my sword, put it up again, made my reverence to my master's guest, asked him in his own language how he did, and told him *he was welcome,* just as my little nurse had instructed me.

This man, who was old and dim-sighted, put on his glasses to see me better. At this I could not help laughing very heartily, for his eyes appeared like the full moon shining into a chamber at two windows. Our people, who found out the cause of my mirth, bore me company in laughing, at which the old fellow was fool enough to be angry. He had the name of being a great miser, and, to my misfortune, he well deserved it, by the advice he gave my master, to show me as a sight upon a market day, in the next town, which was half an hour's riding, about two-and-twenty miles from our house.

I guessed there was some mischief abroad, when I observed my master and his friend whispering long together, and sometimes pointing at me. My fears made them fancy that I over-

heard and understood some of their words. But the next morning Glumdalclitch, my little nurse, told me the whole matter, which she had cunningly found out from her mother. The poor girl laid me on her bosom, and began weeping with shame and grief. She feared some mischief would happen to me from rude folks, who might squeeze me to death, or break one of my limbs by taking me in their hands.

She had also observed how modest I was in my nature, how nicely I regarded my honour, and how badly I would feel to be exposed for money as a public show, to the meanest of the people. She said her papa and mamma had promised that Mannikin should be hers; but now she found they meant to serve her as they did last year, when they pretended to give her a lamb, and yet, as soon as it was fat, sold it to a butcher.

For my own part, I may truly affirm, that I was less concerned than my nurse. I had a strong hope, which never left me, that I should one day recover my liberty.

My master, following the advice of his friend, carried me in a box the next market day to the neighbouring town, and took along with him his little daughter, my nurse, behind him. The box was closed on every side, with a little door for me to go in and out, and a few holes to let in air. The girl had been so careful as to put the quilt of her own bed into it for me to lie down on.

However, I was terribly shaken and disturbed in this journey, though it was but of half an hour, for the horse went about forty feet at every step, and trotted so high that the movement was equal to the rising and falling of a ship in a great storm, but much more frequent. My master alighted at an inn which he used to visit. After consulting for some time with the innkeeper, and making some needful preparations, he hired the crier, to give notice through the town of a strange creature to be seen at the sign of the Green Eagle, not so big as a *splacknuck* (an animal in that country, very finely shaped), about six feet long, and in every part of the body like a human creature, and which could speak several words, and perform a hundred amusing tricks.

I was placed upon a table in the largest room of the inn, which might be nearly three hundred feet square. My little nurse stood on a low stool close to the table, to take care of me, and direct what I should do. My master, to avoid a crowd, would suffer only thirty people at a time to see me. I walked about on the table as the girl commanded. She asked me questions, as far as she knew my understanding of the language reached, and I answered them as loudly as I could.

I turned about several times to the company, paid my humble respects, said *they were welcome,* and used some other speeches I had been taught. I took up a thimble filled with drink, which Glum-dalclitch had given me for a cup, and drank their health. I drew out my sword, and flourished it after the manner of fencers in England.

My nurse gave me a part of a straw, which I exercised as a pike, having learnt the art in my youth. I was that day shown to twelve sets of company, and as often forced to act over again the same things, till I was half-dead with weariness and vexation. Those who had seen me made such wonderful reports, that the people were ready to break down the doors to come in.

My master, for his own interest, would not suffer anyone to touch me except my nurse, and, to prevent danger, benches were set round the table at such distance as put me out of everybody's reach. However, an unlucky schoolboy aimed a hazel nut directly at my head, which very narrowly missed me. It came with so much violence that it would have knocked out my brains, for it was almost as large as a small pumpkin. But I had the satisfaction to see the young rogue well beaten, and turned out of the room.

My master gave public notice that he would show me again the next market day. In the meantime he prepared a more convenient vehicle for me, which he had reason enough to do. I was so tired by my first journey, and by amusing company for eight hours together, that I could hardly stand upon my legs, or speak a word. It was at least three days before I recovered my strength; and, that I might have no rest at home, all the neighbouring gentlemen from a hundred miles round, hearing of my fame, came to see me at my master's own house.

My master, finding how profitable I was likely to be, resolved to carry me to the largest cities in the kingdom. Having therefore provided himself with all things needed for a long journey, and settled his affairs at home, he took leave of his wife, and on the 17th of August, 1703, about two months after my arrival, we set out for the metropolis, which was near the middle of that empire, and about three thousand miles distant from our house. My master made his daughter Glumdalclitch ride behind him. She carried me on her lap, in a box tied about her waist.

My master's plan was to show me in all the towns by the way, and to go out of the road, for fifty or a hundred miles, to any village, or person of quality's house, where he might expect custom. We made easy journeys, of not above seven or eight score miles a day: for Glumdalclitch, on purpose to spare me, complained she was tired with the trotting of the horse. She often took me out of my box at my desire, to give me air, and show me the country, but always held me fast by a leading-string. We were ten weeks on our journey, and I was shown in eighteen large towns, besides at many villages, and at the houses of private families.

On the 26th day of October, we arrived in the metropolis. My master took a lodging in the chief street in the city, not far from the royal palace, and put out bills in the usual form, containing an exact account of my person and parts. He hired a large room between three and four hundred feet wide. He provided a table sixty feet in diameter, upon which I was to act my part, and put a fence round it three feet from the edge, and as many high, to prevent my falling over. I was shown ten times a day, to the wonder and satisfaction of all people. I could now speak the language fairly well, and perfectly understood every word that was spoken to me. Besides, I had learnt their alphabet, and could make a shift to explain a sentence, here and there.

3   GULLIVER GOES TO COURT

The frequent labours I underwent every day made, in a few weeks, a very great change in my health. The more my master got by me the more he wished to get. I could not take my food, and was almost reduced to a skeleton. The farmer,

This obligation was amply repaid by the gain he had made in showing me through half the kingdom, and the price he had now sold me for.

This was the sum of my speech, delivered with great hesitation.

The Queen, giving great allowance for my difficulty in speaking, was, however, surprised at so much wit and good sense in so small an animal. She took me in her own hand, and carried me to the King, who was then in his own chamber. His Majesty, not well observing my shape at first view, asked the Queen, after a cold manner, 'how long it was since she grew fond of a *splacknuck*?' For such, it seems, he took me to be, as I lay upon my breast in Her Majesty's right hand.

But when he heard my voice, and found what I delivered to be regular and rational, he could not hide his surprise.

He desired the Queen to order that care should be taken of me.

The Queen commanded her own cabinet-maker to make a box, that might serve me for a bedchamber. This man, according to my direction, in three weeks finished for me a wooden chamber of sixteen feet square, and twelve high, with sash-windows, a door, and two closets, like a London bed-chamber. The board that made the top was to be lifted up and down by two hinges, to put in a bed ready furnished by Her Majesty's upholsterer, which Glumdalclitch took out every day to air, made with her own hands, and, letting down at night, locked up the roof over me.

A nice workman, who was famous for little curiosities, undertook to make me two chairs, with backs and frames, of a substance not unlike ivory, and two tables, with a cabinet to put my things in. The room was quilted on all sides, as well as the floor and the roof, to prevent any accident from the carelessness of those who carried me, and to break the force of a jolt, when I went in a coach.

I desired a lock for my door, to prevent rats and mice coming in. The smith, after several attempts, made the smallest that ever was seen among them, but I have known a larger at the gate of a gentleman's house in England. I made a shift to keep the key in a pocket of my own, fearing Glumdalclitch might lose it.

The Queen became so fond of my company that she could not dine without me. I had a table placed upon the same table at which Her Majesty ate, just at her elbow, and a chair to sit on. Glumdalclitch stood on a stool on the floor near my table to assist and take care of me. I had an entire set of silver dishes and plates, and other necessaries, which, in proportion to those of the

Queen, were not much bigger than what I have seen in a London toyshop, for the furniture of a doll's-house. These my little nurse kept in her pocket in a silver box, and gave me at meals as I wanted them, always cleaning them herself.

No person dined with the Queen but the two princesses royal, the eldest sixteen years old, and the younger at that time thirteen and a month. Her Majesty used to put a bit of meat upon one of my dishes, out of which I carved for myself, and her amusement was to see me eat. For the Queen (who had indeed but a weak stomach) took up, at one mouthful, as much as a dozen English farmers could eat at a meal, which to me, was for some time a very nasty sight. She would crunch the wing of a lark, bones and all, between her teeth, although it were nine times as large as that of a full-grown turkey; and put a bit of bread in her mouth, as big as two twelve-penny loaves.

She drank out of a golden cup, above a hogshead at a draught. Her knives were twice as long as a scythe, set straight upon the handle. The spoons, forks, and other instruments were all in the same proportion. I remember when Glumdalclitch carried me, out of curiosity, to see some of the tables at Court, where ten or a dozen of those large knives and forks were lifted up together, I thought I had never till then beheld so terrible a sight.

After having been accustomed several months to the sight and talk of this people, and having observed every object upon which I cast mine eyes to be of very large size, the horror I had at first felt from their size and aspect so far wore off. And if I had then beheld a company of English lords and ladies in their finery and birthday clothes, acting their parts in the most courtly manner of strutting, and bowing, and talking, to say the truth, I should have been strongly tempted to laugh as much at them as the King and his grandees did at me.

Neither, indeed, could I forbear smiling at myself, when the Queen used to place me upon her hand towards a looking-glass, by which both our persons appeared before me in full view together. There could be nothing more funny than the comparison. So that I really began to imagine myself dwindled many degrees below my usual size.

Nothing vexed and angered me so much as the Queen's dwarf. He being the smallest person ever seen in that country (for I verily think he was not full thirty feet high), became so impudent at seeing a creature so much beneath him, that he would always affect to swagger and look big as he passed by me in the Queen's antechamber, while I was standing on some table talking with the lords or ladies of the Court. And he seldom failed of a smart word or two upon my littleness. Against this I could only revenge myself by calling him brother, challenging him to wrestle, and such smart sayings as are usually in the mouths of Court pages.

One day, at dinner, this wicked little cub was so annoyed with something I had said to him, that, raising himself upon the frame of Her Majesty's chair, he took me up by the middle, as I was sitting down, not thinking any harm, and let me drop into a large silver bowl of cream, and then ran away as fast as he could. I fell over head and ears, and if I had not been a good swimmer it might have gone very hard with me. But my little nurse ran to my relief, and took me out, after I had swallowed above a quart of cream.

I was put to bed. However, I received no other damage than the loss of a suit of clothes, which was utterly spoiled. The dwarf was soundly whipped, and, as a further punishment, forced to drink up the bowl of cream into which he had thrown me; neither was he ever restored to favour.

I was frequently rallied by the Queen for being so much afraid. She used to ask me whether the

8   (H 757)

people of my country were as great cowards as myself. The occasion was this. The kingdom was much troubled with flies in the summer. These hateful insects, each of them as big as a lark, hardly gave me any rest while I sat at dinner, with their constant humming and buzzing about mine ears. Sometimes they would fix upon my nose or forehead, where they stung me to the quick, smelling very badly. I could easily trace that sticky matter, which, our naturalists tell us, enables those creatures to walk with their feet upwards upon a roof.

I had much ado to defend myself against these hateful animals, and could not forbear starting when they came on my face. It was the common practice of the dwarf to catch a number of these insects in his hand, as schoolboys do among us, and then let them out suddenly under my nose, on purpose to frighten me, and amuse the Queen. My cure was to cut them in pieces with my knife, as they flew in the air, my skill in doing which was much admired.

4   GULLIVER LEAVES BROBDINGNAG

I had now been two years in this country. About the beginning of the third, Glumdalclitch and I attended the King and Queen, in a progress to the south coast of the kingdom. I was carried, as usual, in my travelling-box, which, as I have already described, was a very convenient closet twelve feet wide.

When we came to our journey's end, the King

thought proper to pass a few days at a palace he
has near Flanflasnic, a city within eighteen
English miles of the seaside. Glumdalclitch and I
were very tired. I had got a slight cold, but the
poor girl was so ill as to be confined to her
chamber. I longed to see the ocean, which must
be the only way of my escape, if ever it should
happen.

I pretended to be worse than I really was, and
desired leave to take the fresh air of the sea, with
a page whom I was very fond of, and who had
sometimes been trusted with me. I shall never
forget with what unwillingness Glumdalclitch
consented, or the strict charge she gave the page
to be careful of me, bursting at the same time into
a flood of tears, as if she had some idea of what
was to happen.

The boy took me out in my box, about half
an hour's walk from the palace, towards the rocks
on the seashore. I ordered him to set me down,
and, lifting up one of my sashes, cast many a
wistful look towards the sea. I found myself not
very well, and told the page that I had a mind to
take a nap in my hammock, which I hoped
would do me good. I got in, and the boy shut
the window close down to keep out the cold.

I soon fell asleep, and all I can guess is, while I
slept, the page, thinking no danger could happen,

went among the rocks to look for birds' eggs, having before observed him from my window searching about, and picking up one or two in the clefts. Be that as it may, I found myself suddenly awaked by a violent pull upon the ring, which was fastened at the top of my box, for the convenience of carriage. I felt my box raised very high in the air, and then borne forward with great speed.

The first jolt was like to shake me out of my hammock, but afterwards the motion was easy enough. I called out several times as loud as I could raise my voice, but all to no purpose. I looked towards my windows, and could see nothing but the clouds and sky. I heard a noise just over my head like the clapping of wings, and then began to perceive the sad condition I was in. Some eagle had got the ring of my box in his beak, with an intent to let it fall on a rock, like a tortoise in a shell, and then pick out my body, and devour it; for the cleverness and smell of this bird enable him to discover his prey at a great distance, though better hidden than I could be within a two-inch board.

In a little time I observed the noise and flutter of wings to increase very fast, and my box was tossed up and down like a sign on a windy day. I heard several bangs or buffets, as I thought, given

to the eagle (for such I am certain it must have
been that held the ring of my box in his beak), and
then, all of a sudden, felt myself falling down, for
above a minute, but with such great swiftness
that I almost lost my breath.

My fall was stopped by a terrible splash, that
sounded louder to my ears than the falls of
Niagara. After this I was quite in the dark for
another minute, and then my box began to rise
so high that I could see light from the tops of the
windows. I now saw I was fallen into the sea. My
box, by the weight of my body, the goods that
were in, and the broad plate of iron fixed for
strength at the four corners of the top and
bottom, floated about five feet deep in water.

I did then, and do now, suppose that the eagle
which flew away with my box was pursued by
two or three others, and forced to let me drop,
while he defended himself against the rest, who
hoped to share in the prey. The plates of iron
fastened at the bottom of the box (for those were
the strongest) preserved the balance while it fell,
and hindered it from being broken on the surface
of the water. Every joint of it was well grooved;
and the door did not move on hinges, but up and
down like a sash, which kept my closet so tight
that very little water came in. I got with much
difficulty out of my hammock, having first drawn

back the slipboard on the roof already mentioned, made on purpose to let in air, for want of which I found myself almost stifled.

How often did I then wish myself with my dear Glumdalclitch, from whom one single hour had so far divided me! I was four hours under these circumstances, expecting, and indeed wishing, every moment to be my last. Being in this sad state I heard, or at least thought I heard, some kind of grating noise on that side of my box where the staples were fixed for carrying it. Soon after I began to fancy that the box was pulled or towed along the sea. I now and then felt a sort of tugging, which made the waves rise near the tops of my windows, leave me almost in the dark. This gave me some faint hopes of relief, although I was not able to think how it could be brought about.

I ventured to unscrew one of my chairs, which were always fastened to the floor. Having made a hard shift to screw it down again, directly under the slipping-board that I had lately opened, I mounted on the chair, and, putting my mouth as near as I could to the hole, I called for help in a loud voice, and in all the languages I understood. I then fastened my handkerchief to a stick I usually carried, and, thrusting it up the hole, waved it several times in the air, that if any boat or ship were near, the seamen might think some unhappy mortal was shut up in the box.

I found no effect from all I could do, but plainly perceived my closet to be moved along. In the space of an hour, or better, that side of the box where the staples were, and which had no windows, struck against something that was hard. I feared it was a rock, and found myself tossed more than ever. I plainly heard a noise upon the cover of my closet, like that of a cable, and the grating of it as it passed through the ring. I then found myself hoisted up by degrees, at least three feet higher than I was before.

Upon this I again thrust up my stick and handkerchief, calling for help till I was almost hoarse. In return to these cries I heard a great shout repeated three times, giving me such feelings of joy as are not to be thought of but by those who feel them. I now heard a trampling over my head, and somebody calling through the hole with a loud voice, in the English tongue, that if there was anybody below, he was to speak. I answered I was an Englishman drawn by ill fortune into the greatest calamity that ever any creature underwent, and begged, by all that was moving, to be delivered out of the prison I was in.

The voice replied that I was safe, for my box

was fastened to their ship. The carpenter should immediately come and saw a hole in the cover, large enough to pull me out. I answered that that was needless, and would take up too much time. There was no more to be done, but to let one of the crew put his finger into the ring, and take the box out of the sea into the ship, and so into the captain's cabin. Some of them, upon hearing me talk so wildly, thought I was mad. Others laughed. Indeed it never came into my head that I was now among people of my own size and strength. The carpenter came, and in a few minutes sawed a passage of about four feet square, then let down a small ladder, upon which I mounted, and thence was taken into the ship in a very weak condition.

The sailors were all in amazement, and asked me a thousand questions which I had no desire to answer. But the captain, Mr. Thomas Wilcocks, an honest, worthy Shropshire man, observing I was ready to faint, took me into his cabin, gave me a cordial to comfort me, and made me turn in upon his own bed, advising me to take a little rest, of which I had great need.

Upon waking I found myself much recovered. It was now about eight o'clock at night, and the captain ordered supper immediately, thinking I had already fasted too long. He entertained me with great kindness, observing me not to look wildly or talk foolishly. When we were left alone, he desired I would give him an account of my travels, and by what accident I came to be set adrift in that huge wooden chest.

I begged his patience to hear me tell my story, which I faithfully did, from the last time I left England to the moment he first discovered me. And as truth always forces its way into rational minds, so this honest, worthy gentleman, who had some learning, and very good sense, was immediately convinced of the truth I spoke.

Our voyage was very prosperous, but I shall not trouble the reader with a journal of it. I left the ship when we came into the Downs, which was on the third day of June, 1706, about nine months after my escape.